OUR CAT FLOSSIE

1 3 5 7 9 0 8 6 4 2

First published in the United Kingdom 1986 by Andersen Press

First published in Mini Treasures edition 1998
by Red Fox
Random House, 20 Vauxhall Bridge Road,
London, SW1V 2SA

Random House Australia (Pty) Ltd
20 Alfred Street, Milsons Point, Sydney,
New South Wales 2061, Australia

Random House New Zealand Limited
18 Poland Road, Glenfield,
Auckland 10, New Zealand

Random House South Africa
PO Box 2263, Rosebank 2121, South Africa

RANDOM HOUSE UK Limited Reg No. 954009

A CIP catalogue record for this book is available
from the British library.
Printed in Singapore

ISBN 0 099 26343 2

OUR CAT FLOSSIE

Ruth Brown

Mini Treasures

RED FOX

This is our cat Flossie.

She lives with us in London.

She likes the house and the garden,
but does not get on very well
with the neighbours.

Her hobbies include birdwatching –

and fishing.

Flossie is a skilful climber and

an extremely enthusiastic gardener.

She always insists on helping
with knitting

and making the beds.

She is very good at polishing shoes

but not quite so useful at
Christmas-time.

There are two things which she hates –
the sound of fireworks

and visits to the vet.

Flossie loves collecting butterflies

and she is rather fond of snails

even though she finds them
puzzling.

She is unable to resist a box

no matter what the size.

But, like all cats, most of all
she loves to sleep...

and sleep . . .

and sleep.